This book is dedicated to every child and adult who has ever felt different or not good enough. You can have the life you want and deserve because you have the tools to attain it. You are perfectly designed . . . and please never forget that.
—Love, K.B. and J.B.

For my sweet nephew Mikael.
—A.S.

Henry Holt and Company, *Publishers since 1866*
Henry Holt® is a registered trademark of Macmillan Publishing Group, LLC
120 Broadway, New York, New York 10271 • mackids.com

Text copyright © 2019 by Karamo Brown
Illustrations copyright © 2019 by Anoosha Syed
All rights reserved.

Library of Congress Control Number 2019932421
ISBN 978-1-250-23221-2

Our books may be purchased in bulk for promotional, educational, or business use.
Please contact your local bookseller or the Macmillan Corporate and Premium Sales Department
at (800) 221-7945 ext. 5442 or by email at MacmillanSpecialMarkets@macmillan.com.

First edition, 2019 / Design by Mallory Grigg
The illustrations for this book were created digitally.
Printed in China by RR Donnelley Asia Printing Solutions Ltd.,
Dongguan City, Guangdong Province
10 9 8 7 6 5 4 3 2 1

I Am
Perfectly Designed

Karamo Brown and Jason "Rachel" Brown

Illustrated by Anoosha Syed

Henry Holt and Company • New York

First there was you, Dad.

Then there was me.

And now there is us!

That's right.
Now there is us.

When you first saw me, you said,

"He is perfectly designed, from his head to his toes."

And I meant every word. Still do.

When I was a baby, I looked just like you . . .
Only I had no hair, and you had lots.

Now . . . it's the opposite.

So true.

The first thing I remember is being
carried on your shoulders while you walked me all over the city.

Remember that?
I had such a big baby head!

Indeed.

**But your big baby
head was perfectly
designed for you.**

When I was real little, I thought
you could touch the moon. Remember that?
We'd sit on the roof and reach for it.

One day, you'll be big enough to reach it yourself.

But until then, it's perfectly fine to ask for help.

Remember when we went as syrup and waffles for Halloween, Dad?

Ha! I do, I do.

That was awesome.
I wonder what
we'll be this year!

When I run in the park,

jump in the park,

climb trees in the park,

and pretend I am a
statue in the park,
you remind me I am perfectly
designed to explore the world.

You are, and you always will be.

Sometimes, Dad,
when I get mad,

or sad,

or confused,

you wrap me in your arms.
I like that.

Me, too.
And I remind you that you are
perfectly designed and wonderful.
No matter what you're feeling.

Dad . . . when I grow up and leave home—
will you miss me?

Yes. Very much.

Will you go into my room and play
with my race cars and stuffed animals?

You know I will!

Will you sit on the fire
escape and feed the pigeons
like we do in the summer?

The pigeons *and* the sparrows.

Will you remember our favorite moves?

I will, and I'll invent some new ones, too.

Dad . . . will you always think of me?

Always.

You know what, Dad?

What?

I will always remember walking through the city
and sitting on your shoulders.
And maybe when you're older, and I'm taller . . .

. . . I can carry you on mine,
because we are perfectly designed for each other.

That's right.

Dear Reader,

It's always been a dream of mine to write a story inspired by the many lessons my father has taught me. When I was growing up, anytime I felt fear or uncertainty, my father would remind me that I was perfectly designed.

Knowing that at an early age really instilled self-love and confidence in me, which had been hard to find on my own. Now that I'm older, it's easier to walk with my head held up proudly. My father and I felt it was only right to give this message to you.

We want readers to never forget that just being your natural self is perfect. It's beautiful in every sense. We know how hard it is to think otherwise, but you can't stop telling yourself this until you feel it! Like everything in life, it takes some time. But with repetition, you will learn to walk with your head held higher than the Eiffel Tower.

—Jason Brown

That's exactly right.

—Karamo Brown